Designed by Nicola Butler

Usborne House, 83-85 Saffron Hill, London EC1N 8RT, England

I'm NOT (very) AFRAID of the DARK

Anna Milbourne

Illustrated by
Daniel Rieley

I tell everyone that I'm not scared of **anything**.
Poisonous snakes? Not likely!
Giant, hairy spiders? Never!

"Are you afraid of the dark?" they ask.

"NO," I say.
(But I think,
"Not _very_...")

Well, at least it's true in the daytime.

In the day, the Dark is small. It tucks itself
under things, almost as if it's hiding.

But as the sun goes down,
the Dark stretches out.
It gets bigger...

...and bigger,
and starts to cover
EVERYTHING.

And the feeling
inside me gets bigger too –
like a hole I could fall into.

Nobody knows
about it but me.

MY ROOM –
MONSTERS
KEEP OUT!

When I'm inside my house with the lights on, everything's bright and cosy... Mostly.

But there are corners where the Dark lurks...

...and
shadows
on the
stairs.

The feeling vanishes as I'm getting ready for bed.
It's swallowed up by the bedtime bustle.

It's all busy-busy:

Pyjamas on.

Brush my teeth.

Tuck Ted in.

Then comes story time, all snuggly and warm.

But all too soon, it's,
"Goodnight, sleep tight!" And...

CLICK!

Off
goes
the
light...

In the stillness of the Dark,
I start to notice things I didn't see before.

Monster-y shapes on the wall...

A tap-tap-tap
at the window...

SOMETHING
creeping across
the floor...!

QUICK-
switch on the light!

There was NOTHING scary there at all!

Just shadows of my toys - old Anteater, cuddly Croc and Olly Octopus...

...some branches
waving in the wind...

...a tangle
of clothes
on the floor.

What was there
to be afraid of?

Then one day, Dad says, "Let's go camping." And off we go. But silently I wonder if the Dark will find me there TOO.

The scared feeling vanishes as we're putting up the tent. It's all busy-busy: pick a good spot; in go the tent pegs, with a bang-bang-BANG....

We unroll our sleeping bags, all cosy in the lamplight.

And, before I've thought of it, the Dark's already come.

But out here, the Dark is huge
and wide, and more of an adventure.
I decide it's like a guessing game.

What's that swishy-swishing?

Just the trees in the breeze.

A shadow and a glimmer of eyes?

Only an owl.

Flitter-flutter...?

Moths!

Do I *dare switch off my light...?* **I do!**
And that's when **I** *discover the most magical thing of all...*

It's only when it's REALLY DARK
that I can see all the stars.

In the morning,
the light comes back.
It spills over everything,
and covers up the stars.

And so I wonder...
Maybe the **Dark** isn't all that bad?

It's just a big,
velvety night-blanket,
wrapped around the world
so it can go to sleep.

And if the **Dark** never came, you'd never, ever see the stars.

In the end, I told my mum all about my feelings.
And she said it's okay – I can leave my lamp on anyway.
So... am I still afraid of the Dark?

Maybe sometimes,
just a little...

But when I think of all those stars,
sometimes the feeling melts away.
And I feel brave enough to switch off my light...

Goodnight!